27634

S0-BHT-019

Put Beginning Readers on the Right Track with
ALL ABOARD READING™

The All Aboard Reading series is especially for beginning readers. Written by noted authors and illustrated in full color, these are books that children really and truly *want* to read—books to excite their imagination, tickle their funny bone, expand their interests, and support their feelings. With four different reading levels, All Aboard Reading lets you choose which books are most appropriate for your children and their growing abilities.

Picture Readers—for Ages 3 to 6
Picture Readers have super-simple texts, with many nouns appearing as rebus pictures. At the end of each book are 24 flash cards—on one side is the rebus picture; on the other side is the written-out word.

Level 1—for Preschool through First-Grade Children
Level 1 books have very few lines per page, very large type, easy words, lots of repetition, and pictures with visual "cues" to help children figure out the words on the page.

Level 2—for First-Grade to Third-Grade Children
Level 2 books are printed in slightly smaller type than Level 1 books. The stories are more complex, but there is still lots of repetition in the text, and many pictures. The sentences are quite simple and are broken up into short lines to make reading easier.

Level 3—for Second-Grade through Third-Grade Children
Level 3 books have considerably longer texts, harder words, and more complicated sentences.

All Aboard for happy reading!

For Ethel, for teaching me to love books and for teaching
me the complexities and joy of being a woman.
For David, for teaching me never to settle and for
forming my standards of what makes a good man.
For Jon, the real writer in the family,
for the lessons of perseverance.
For Linda, for the gift she gave me back in 1971.
And for the men in my life, Lance and Luke, your
mere existence is a triumph over great odds. You are
my anchor, my passion, my path, my heart.
—Kristin Armstrong

Dedicated to all that have overcome obstacles to reach their
goals in life.—Ken Call

Photo credits: front cover, Tom Able-Green/Allsport; back cover, Baron Erik Spafford;
p. 3, Doug Pensinger/Allsport; p. 4, courtesy of Linda Armstrong; p. 5, courtesy of Linda
Armstrong; p. 9, 13, 19, 24, 33, 38, Doug Pensinger/Allsport; p. 16, Graham Watson;
p. 20, Doug Pensinger/Allsport; p. 23, Mike Powell/Allsport; p. 27, courtesy of Linda
Armstrong; p. 29, courtesy of Linda Armstrong; p. 30, courtesy of Kristin Armstrong; p. 31,
Baron Erik Spafford; p. 32, courtesy of Linda Armstrong; p. 35, Graham Watson; p. 37, Mike
Powell/Allsport; p. 39, Mike Powell/Allsport; p. 41, Stephane Kempinaire/Allsport; p. 42, Doug
Pensinger/Allsport; p. 44, Doug Pensinger/Allsport; p. 46, James Startt; p. 47, courtesy of Linda
Armstrong; p. 48, Baron Erik Spafford

Text copyright © 2000 by Kristin Armstrong. Illustrations copyright © 2000 by Ken Call. All
rights reserved. Published by Grosset & Dunlap, a division of Penguin Putnam Books for
Young Readers, New York. GROSSET & DUNLAP and ALL ABOARD READING are
trademarks of Penguin Putnam Inc. Published simultaneously in Canada. Printed in the U.S.A.

Library of Congress Cataloging-in-Publication Data is available.

ISBN 0-448-42415-0 (GB) A B C D E F G H I J
ISBN 0-448-42407-X (pbk) A B C D E F G H I J

ALL
ABOARD
READING™

Level 3
Grades 2-3

Lance Armstrong
The Race of His Life

By Kristin Armstrong
Illustrated by Ken Call
With photographs

Grosset & Dunlap • New York

Lance and the Pink Jacket

There once was a boy named Lance Armstrong. He was born on September 18, 1971, and grew up in Plano, Texas. Lance was an only child, and lived with his mom.

Like lots of kids, Lance liked sports. He liked to swim. He liked to run. Most of all, he liked to ride his bike.

Lance got his first bike when he was about seven. It was an ugly brown bike with yellow wheels. But Lance loved it.

On his bike, he could go anywhere. He was free.

He rode around with his friends after school. He rode all day on weekends. Everywhere he went, he rode his bike.

Lance became very strong. Pretty soon he could ride faster and farther than all his friends. Then he could ride faster and farther than anybody in his whole school. Then he could even ride faster and farther than many adults! One day he rode and rode, and guess where he ended up. Oklahoma! That's a whole state away. It was getting dark, so his mom had to pick him up in the car and drive him home.

Lance, at 9, with his uncle and his brand-new bike

Lance decided that he would enter some bike races. His mom drove him to the races on the weekends.

One race was far from home in New Mexico. The trip took two days by car.

On the morning of the big race, Lance got up and put on his racing clothes—a cycling jersey, shorts, and special shoes that clip on to the pedals. He went outside the motel. But a second later he came running back in.

"Mom, I can't race in these clothes. It's freezing outside," he said.

His mom got out of bed and stepped outside. Lance was right. It <u>was</u> freezing.

They were used to hot weather in Texas, and they didn't know it would be so cold.

"Son," she said, "we don't have anything else for you to wear. I'm sorry."

Then she handed him the only jacket she brought on the trip.

"Here, honey. You can borrow this."

The jacket was pink and several sizes too small. He had no choice but to put it on. After he zipped it up, Lance couldn't even move his arms.

Before the race, the cyclists were riding around, trying to warm up. They had fancy bikes and nice clothes. They

wondered who the strange boy was in the shabby pink jacket.

The cyclists took their places at the starting line. Lance took off the pink jacket and was ready to go.

His mom said, "Good luck, son. Hurry up and win because your mama's cold."

The gun sounded, and they were off!

Lance passed the first group of guys with the nice clothes. Then he passed the guys with the nice bikes. Finally he passed the guys who had been staring at the kid in the pink jacket, and guess what. He won the race! His mom was very proud.

"You see, son," she said, "you don't have to have expensive things to be a winner. You have to think like a winner and believe you can win…and you will."

Lance Goes to Europe

For most kids, riding a bike is just something fun to do. It's also a way to get from one place to another. But for Lance, bike riding became a serious sport.

Just like football and baseball, bike racing has teams. When Lance was sixteen, he was asked to be on a team.

Lance won bike races all over the United States, and people began to learn his name. In Europe, bike racing is one of the most popular sports. The best cyclists in the world live and race in Europe.

Lance's coaches said, "If you want to race with the best, you will have to race in Europe."

So Lance moved to Italy. He was only eighteen years old. But the coach of his new team was Italian, and Lance wanted to live near him. Lance had just enough money for a small apartment. At first, Lance didn't speak any Italian. No one spoke any English, either! Lance was very lonely.

His very first race in Europe was in Spain, in a town called San Sebastian. Lance thought he could win, but he was in for a big surprise. Racing in Europe was much harder than he thought! Lance finished in last place. He was embarrassed and thought about going back to the U.S.

But, instead he trained harder, riding in the mountains. He kept racing even though he wasn't the best. He watched

the older riders and learned how to help his teammates.

Teammates do different things to help one another. Some riders bring food and water to the riders who are in the front of the pack. Other riders ride in front and try to block the wind for the teammates who are right behind them. No matter what, teammates always stick together.

Slowly Lance learned to speak Italian. He made some friends. One special friend was a guy named Fabio Casartelli. Fabio was a great racer. He was the pride of his village. But he also loved to have fun and joke around. Having Fabio for a friend really helped.

The next year, when it was time to race in San Sebastian again, Lance was ready. This time, he won!

Lance Meets the King

Each fall, the World Championships are held in Europe. This is an important bike race. It is one day long, and the winner is called the best cyclist in the entire world.

Ever since Lance was a little boy, he always wanted to be the very best at something. When he was twenty-one, he decided to become the best cyclist. He worked very hard to reach his goal. Every day he would ride for five hours or more.

Lance had no time for fun. All he did was train. After he rode his bike, he would eat pasta and go to sleep. Then he would get up the next day and do the same thing. Over and over, for many weeks, he trained hard to be the best.

Lance looked for the steepest hills and the longest paths. He rode in the rain and in the cold. He never missed one day of training.

The day of the big race was on August 29, 1993. Lance was ready. The race was in Norway, and it was very difficult. It was more than 160 miles long! The weather was cold and rainy. But Lance was glad. He thought the bad weather might make other people give up.

For most of the day, Lance stayed near the front of the peloton. (You say it like this: pell-low-TON.) Peloton is a French word that means the group of cyclists in a race. Toward the end of the race, Lance knew it was time to break away. That means getting ahead of the rest of the peloton and trying to win.

So that's what he did. He broke away. The other cyclists tried to chase him. The rain was pouring down, and it was hard to see. Lance's legs pumped harder and harder, more than 90 times a minute. He was biking at 40 miles an hour! That is as fast as a car. Lance was in the lead, and no one could catch him.

He crossed the finish line first and was the new champion of the world! Everyone was amazed because he was the youngest winner ever.

World champion Lance in Oslo, Norway in 1993

The world champion gets a gold medal and a special shirt with a rainbow on it. It is a very big honor to wear the rainbow jersey. It means that you are the best.

Lance was invited to the palace of the king of Norway. He was going to meet the king and get his medal and his rainbow jersey. Lance's mom came with him, and they both were very excited.

When Lance and his mom got to the front door, the guard told Lance that he was the only one allowed to enter. His mom would have to wait outside.

For Lance's whole life, his mom had helped him in any way she could. She had taken him to many races when he was just a boy. She had helped him buy his first bike. Lance thought about all these things.

He told the guard, "No, thank you. If my mom can't come, I'm not going." And he turned to walk away.

A few minutes later, the guard came running after them.

"Wait! Don't leave! The king wants to meet you both," he said.

So Lance and his mom both went inside the palace. The king presented Lance with his gold medal and his rainbow jersey. His mom was there to see it. She was awfully proud.

Lance Loses a Friend

Of all bike races, the Tour de France is the biggest and most famous. Teams come from all over the world. The race lasts the whole month of July and travels all over France. The Tour is 2,500 miles long. The cyclists have to bike about five hours a day.

Some days the course is in flat valleys.

Other days the course goes up steep, snowy mountains.

Some days it is sunny and nice.

Other days the cyclists have to ride in snow or icy rain.

People line the streets when the Tour de France passes through their towns. They scream and cheer for the cyclists. The fans are always there, no matter if it's sunny or snowing.

The race is very hard. Only the strongest riders can finish. The rider with the fastest time wins the Tour de France, but no person can win the Tour de

Lance's team car following him at the Tour de France

France alone. Just like other races, riding and winning the tour takes strong teamwork.

Each day, team cars and motorcycles follow the riders. Team cars are painted in team colors, with extra bicycles on the roof in case someone gets a flat tire. Mechanics ride in the backseat in case they have to make repairs along the way. The motorcycles usually carry people with cameras who take photos for newspapers all over the world.

In 1995, Lance's team was doing well in the Tour de France.

After fourteen days of racing, the peloton was deep in the mountains of France. Right as he came down a steep hill, Lance heard a terrible noise in front of him. Cyclists, team cars, and motorcycles all screeched to a stop.

It could mean only one thing—an accident. A bad accident. It was one of Lance's teammates, his good friend Fabio Casartelli. Fabio had crashed into a cement wall. His bike was a wreck. Doctors put Fabio on a stretcher. But it was too late. Fabio was dead.

The race was over for the rest of the awful day. Lance and his whole team were in shock. No one could speak. They thought about quitting the Tour because they were so sad.

But the next day, the team was back. They knew that Fabio would want them to keep going. So they rode in his honor, and they rode hard. That day, Lance worked harder than he ever had in his life. He flew past other riders until he was finally alone in front of the peloton.

Something strange happened in the last stretch of the race. Lance could feel Fabio with him. With Fabio's help, he rode so fast, no one could catch him.

As Lance sailed over the finish line alone, he held his arms straight up and pointed at the sky. It was his way of thanking his friend Fabio.

This one's for Fabio

Lance Gets Sick

The year 1996 was a great one for Lance Armstrong. He was winning races. He was feeling strong. Everyone thought he was on his way to the top.

He came home to Austin, Texas, to celebrate his twenty-fifth birthday. Right after his birthday party, he started feeling sick. First it was some bad headaches. Pretty soon his whole body started to ache. It was his body's way of telling Lance to get to a doctor—quick!

It didn't take long before the doctor found out what was wrong.

"Lance," he said, "I have some very serious news for you. You have cancer and it is spreading all over your body. There are even some spots in your lungs." Lance looked at the X-rays. There was no way to deny it. Lance was very sick.

Lance was afraid, but he was going to do whatever the doctor told him to do. More than anything, Lance wanted to live.

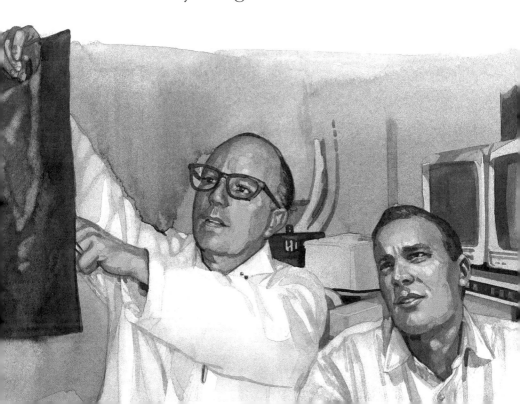

He called his mom and his friends to share the bad news. His mom was sad and very afraid, but she tried to be strong to help Lance. People were very surprised that someone so young and healthy and strong could suddenly be so sick. But that is how cancer is. It hides inside people as it grows.

That night, Lance sat by the pool outside his house and thought about how much he loved being alive. He decided that he would fight cancer, harder than he had ever fought in any race in his life. He told himself that he was never going to give up.

Lance and his mom learned that the best doctors for his kind of cancer were in Indianapolis, Indiana. So they got on a plane and flew there. Soon the doctors had a plan for Lance.

The plan was to get rid of the cancer as quickly as possible. To do so, they used special cancer-fighting drugs. The drugs can make you throw up. And they sometimes make your hair fall out. But Lance didn't care. He wanted to live, so he took the drugs. He did go bald, but so what!

For a while it seemed like the drugs were working. Then one day Lance got

Lance with one of his doctors

more bad news. Doctors found that the cancer had spread to Lance's brain.

When Lance learned that he had cancer in his brain, he was more scared and more unhappy than he ever had been in his life. He didn't know if he could take any more bad news. But he remembered his promise to himself that he would never give up. So he tried to be brave.

Lance had an operation. The doctors took the cancer out of his brain. Soon Lance started to feel better. He went back to Indiana each month for more cancer-fighting drugs. They made him so sick that the only thing he could eat was apple fritters! Whenever he felt really bad, he would smile to himself. He knew that the cancer cells were feeling worse. The drugs were killing the bad cells and saving Lance's life.

After he finished the last dose of the drugs, Lance flew back home. Several days later he went to his doctor for a check-up. His blood tests showed that the cancer was gone! Just to be safe, Lance went for a check-up every month.

Lance at Christmastime in 1996

While Lance was in Austin, he met a new friend named Kristin. She went with him to every doctor appointment. Lance liked having Kristin around because she made him very happy. She made him laugh, even when he was afraid. They told each other all their secrets, and soon they were best friends. She promised she would never leave him, and he believed her.

Lance with Kristin

Lance and Kristin on their wedding day

In October 1997, Lance had his one-year check-up. Everything was all right! He had a huge party to celebrate the good news. Even though Lance was well, he could not forget about the cancer. He could not forget that he had come very close to dying. This experience changed his life in many good ways.

He decided that he would live his life to the fullest. He was going to do everything that was important to him. He and Kristin got married. He told special

31

people how much he loved them. He made lots of time for his family and his friends. And he started raising money for cancer research. He was happier than ever before. His favorite saying became "Carpe Diem!" This is a Latin phrase that means "Seize the day." It means enjoy life and have fun every day.

Lance and his mom

Lance Comes Back

Once Lance was well, he decided he was ready to go back to bicycling. At first he was very tired. He could not ride very fast or very far. He would ride slowly on the hills, and it was hard for him to breathe. His legs were not as strong as they had been, before he got sick. But Lance kept riding. Every day he could ride a little farther than the day before.

His friends would ride with him. "Come on, Lance. You can do it!" they would say. Over time, Lance got stronger and faster. Soon he began to think that he was ready to try racing again. He called his team and told them he was ready to come back to Europe.

But his team didn't want him. They didn't think Lance had what it took. They worried he might get sick again. Lance was fired. He tried calling different teams to see if they would let him join.

"No way." Click.

"You're no good anymore." Click.

"You can't do it." Click.

"Aren't you that sick guy?" Click.

Now Lance started to get really mad. He had worked so hard to fight the cancer that almost killed him. He had worked so hard to ride his bike again. But no one wanted him. No one believed in him anymore. Still, Lance believed in himself.

Lance called an old friend who had a cycling team. The old friend remembered that Lance used to be strong. He believed he could be strong again. Soon Lance joined the U.S. Postal Cycling Team.

Lance on his new team

The cycling season began in Europe. Lance came in fourteenth in his first race. That was pretty good. Everyone was surprised.

At every race, Lance saw people who had said his career was over. He wanted to show them, so he started riding harder and faster than before. He won a race in Luxembourg. Then he won a race in Germany. Then he took fourth place in a hard race in Spain that was a month long.

Finally, in October, Lance won fourth place in the World Championships. Lance wanted to show people who have cancer that they can do anything they want if they put their minds to it.

Lance, strong and fast again

Lance and the Yellow Jersey

After such a good season, some other teams called and wanted Lance to join. But the U.S. Postal Team had given him a chance when no one else would. Lance stayed with the team that had believed in him.

Lance wanted to race in the Tour de France in July 1999. He made that his goal.

Bike racers need to be light when they ride in the mountains. Lance decided that he had to lose weight. So he weighed all of his food on a special scale. He never ate dessert. That wasn't easy—Lance loves dessert!

In the Tour de France, each day is called a "stage." That spring, Lance and Johan, the team boss, traveled to all the towns on the Tour de France map. Every day, Lance would practice one stage. Some days it would snow and hail, but

Lance checking out his bike

Lance never quit. He wore a special microphone in his ear so that Johan could talk to him from the car behind. Johan would say, "Don't stop. You can do this. You can be the best."

Johan helped Lance by making sure he was prepared. He showed him which curves were dangerous and taught him how to save his energy on the mountains. By the time July arrived, Lance was ready to begin the Tour.

The first day of the tour is called the Prologue. During the Prologue, one rider at a time races against the clock. The fastest guy wins. Each rider starts alone on a ramp. One, two, three...Go!

There are time checks along the way. Lance was the fastest rider at every time check on the course! He finished in first place and won the yellow jersey.

Lance in the yellow jersey

Wearing the yellow jersey is the highest honor in the Tour de France. Since no one knew how hard Lance had worked to prepare for the tour, everyone was surprised to see him in yellow.

Days passed. Sometimes Lance kept the yellow jersey, and other days other riders beat him. It was hard work. The next big day for Lance came during Stage 8, in Metz, France. It was another race against the clock. This was Lance's big chance to get the yellow jersey back.

Lance in Metz, France

Once again, he had the fastest time at each check and he won the stage! Lance was in yellow again!

Back in the United States, people started to watch the Tour de France on TV. They knew about a rider named Lance Armstrong. They knew that once he had been sick with cancer. But now he was winning the hardest bike race in the world. People were amazed.

Soon it was time to race in the mountains called the Alps. Some people thought Lance might lose the yellow jersey because he wasn't the best at going up hills. But they didn't know that he had lost weight and practiced riding uphill every day.

The days in the Alps began, and Lance was ready to prove himself. With the help of his teammates, he stayed in the front

Lance giving it his all

for most of the stage. Toward the end of the day, several of the best climbers broke away from the peloton. Lance knew it was now or never. This was his big chance. He rode as hard as he could, and he flew up the mountain, leaving the stunned peloton in the dust!

He finished the stage alone with his arms in the air. He proved he could climb mountains and win.

The final day of the tour is very special. The whole peloton rides together into Paris and finishes on a famous street called the Champs Elysées. (You say it like this: shoms el-ee-say.) There is a big parade and a ceremony to honor the winners.

Lance crossed the finish line with the fastest time in the peloton. He did it! He won the Tour de France!

As Lance rode onto the Champs Elysées, he was draped in an American flag. It was his proudest moment. He later stood on a stage as they played the "Star-Spangled Banner." Many Americans cried tears of joy. His mom was there. So was Kristin. Lance got lots of flowers and

Lance (in hat) with his teammates

Lance with Kristin and his mom

a beautiful trophy. The whole day was a dream come true. Truly, Lance had seized the day. Carpe Diem!

After the Tour de France, everyone said Lance's life could not possibly get any better. But they were wrong.

In October 1999, Lance and Kristin had a little baby boy, a son. His name is Luke Armstrong.

Luke has blue eyes, a big smile, and strong legs. Just like his daddy.

Lance, Luke, and Kristin.

On July 23, 2000 Lance won the Tour de France again. That makes it two in a row!